0 0001 6008248 3

MAIN

P9-DII-885

How I Survived the OREGON TRAIL

THE JOURNAL OF JESSE ADAMS

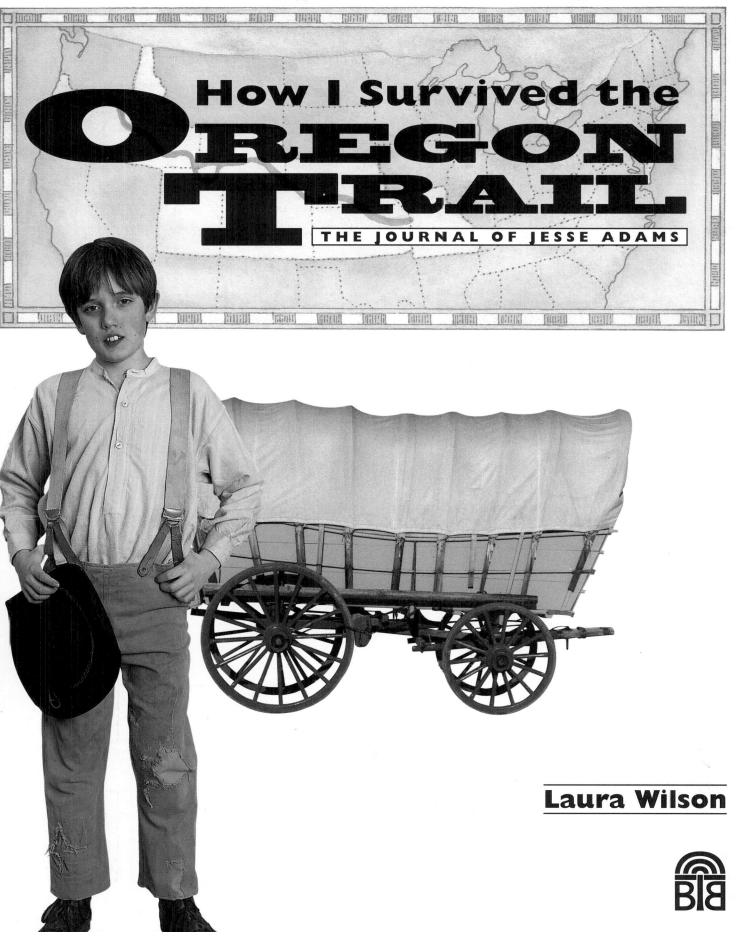

Laura Wilson

A Beech Tree Paperback Book • New York

Volume copyright © 1999 by
Breslich & Foss Ltd.

The author's moral rights have been
asserted.

All rights reserved. No part of this
book may be reproduced or utilized
in any form or by any means,
electronic or mechanical, including
photocopying, recording, or by any
information storage and retrieval
system, without permission in writing
from the Publisher. Inquiries should
be addressed to Beech Tree Books,
a division of William Morrow &
Company, Inc., 1350 Avenue of the
Americas, New York, NY 10019.
www.williammorrow.com

The Library of Congress has cataloged
the Beech Tree Books edition of
How I Survived the Oregon Trail
as follows:

Wilson, Laura, 1964-
How I survived the Oregon Trail: the journal of
Jesse Adams / by Laura Wilson.
p. cm. (Time travelers)
Summary: A young boy keeps a journal
describing his family's five-month journey
across country in a covered wagon.
Each entry includes a game,
recipe, or other related activity.
ISBN 0-688-17276-8
[1. Overland journeys to the Pacific— Fiction.
2. Frontier and pioneer life—West (U.S.)—
Fiction.
3. Oregon Trail—Fiction.]
I. Title. II. Series.
PZ7.W69657Ho   1999
[Fic]—dc21
99-25328   CIP

10 9 8 7 6 5 4 3 2 1

Printed in Italy

First Beech Tree Edition, 1999
ISBN 0-688-17276-8

Conceived and produced by
Breslich & Foss Ltd., London

CONTENTS

Introduction 4

JESSE'S JOURNAL 5

INTRODUCTION

IN the nineteenth century, the United States of America increased in size until it stretched from the Atlantic Ocean to the Pacific. By negotiating, fighting, or buying land, the government acquired the territory that today makes up the states from Kansas and Nebraska to Washington, Oregon, and California. When pioneers had first set out to explore these new lands, they found a vast area of grassland west of the Mississippi River. They called it "the Great American Desert" because few rivers ran across it and there were hardly any trees. Today, this land is known as the Great Plains. When they had crossed the Plains, the explorers came upon the enormous range of the Rocky Mountains. After that, if they traveled north, they had to cross the semidesert of the Columbia Plateau and the Cascade Mountains before reaching the Pacific coastlands. They realized that this was excellent land for farming, with fertile soil and a good climate.

Back east, people began to hear stories about the wonderful land across the Plains. The U.S. Government wanted people to move west, so it began to offer free land to anyone who was willing to travel there. Many farmers were prepared to take the risk, even though it meant traveling over 2,000 miles in ox-drawn wagons. The journey, which took more than five months, was a very dangerous one.

Nobody who survived this amazing journey ever forgot it, and not all of the memories were bad. Many younger pioneers described it as "a continuous picnic" with plenty of fun and games. Some kept diaries during their trip, while others waited until they were comfortably settled in Oregon before writing about their journeys. Although Jesse Adams never existed, the entries in his "diary" are drawn from true accounts of life on the wagon train.

JESSE'S JOURNAL

MY name is Jesse Adams, and I come from Iowa. I am ten years old. My Pa is a farmer. I have two younger sisters. Sarah is eight, and pretty fine for a girl. Martha is three and dull company, although Sarah seems to like her well enough. When Ma told me we would go to Oregon, I begged an old ledger from her to keep a journal of how it was. And you need not turn your nose up at it neither, for it was a mighty fine adventure.

Iowa, February 1852

All the talk at our house is of Oregon. Even Martha is playing that Ma's work basket is a wagon. Ma calls it "Oregon Fever." She does not want us to cross the Plains because of the danger.

Sarah does, though, and so do I. Ma says we'll be taken by the Indians and get behind with our schooling. I don't care. Maybe Pa will let me drive the cattle on the road to Oregon.

All you can hear is the loom banging away as Ma makes our clothes. I got three new shirts and two pairs of pants. Ma said I can have a store-bought hat when we get to St. Joseph. She says Sarah must wear her sunbonnet or she will lose her fair complexion and nobody will marry her. Sarah is helping Ma make preserves and bake as much as she can. I can't even get a taste of the cake mixture, because she shoos me out of the kitchen like I was a chicken. But Pa calls me to help him with the livestock so away I go.

Here is a picture of me.

This is my sister Sarah.

Here is a picture of Ma and Pa.

This is my little sister Martha.

IOWA

WE'RE bound for St. Joseph, Missouri, to meet up with all the folks and start our journey west. It's called "jumping off."

Pa sold the farm easy enough and bought a good wagon from our neighbor. He sold most all of the livestock, save our mare Fan, and Ma's two best milk cows and laying hens. He plans to buy fresh oxen when we get to St. Joseph. Our big wagon can carry 2,500 pounds, and must have four yoke of oxen to pull it.

Pa sold most of our furniture. Some people have two wagons, packed with fine things. Pa says it is foolish to add extra weight to no purpose, but Ma said that she would not leave Iowa without her favorite rocking chair, and so it was tied to the back of the wagon.

Pa packed his farm tools in the wagon, for he has heard there are no such articles to be had in Oregon. Then there are the tents Ma made,

Pa bought a special box to carry some of Ma's cooking things.

Our wagon is ten feet long and four feet wide and looks very fine. Pa hung a tub of grease beneath the wagon to make the wheels run smooth. I wonder how many times they will have to turn before we get to Oregon.

blankets, featherbeds, clothes, and a vast deal of foodstuffs in sacks and bags. Pa's shotgun and lantern are hanging where he can reach them. The wagon looks very handsome. Pa bought a special box for Ma's cooking articles and fixed it onto the side. Then Pa and Ma bought tin cups and plates to put into it. Ma was sad to part with most of her china, but space was found for her best pieces.

It's too bad—Sarah just told me that she saw Ma putting the grammar and the arithmetic books into the wagon.

Ma packs her treasured china plates in barrels of cornmeal so they will not be broken by the jolting of the wagon.

Pa's Arithmetic

If you like figuring, here's how much money Pa spent for our journey:

Wagon = $90

Four yoke of oxen at $50 per yoke = $200

Gear = $100

Tinware, pots, and pans = $20

Food—600 pounds of flour = $12

60 pounds of coffee = $4.20

100 pounds of sugar = $10

200 pounds of beans = $16

40 pounds of salt = $1.60

8 pounds of pepper = 32¢

1 keg of whiskey (only for medicine) = $5

Ma brought 120 pounds of biscuits, 400 pounds of bacon, 200 pounds of lard, 120 pounds of dried fruit, and some pies and preserves from our home in Iowa, so Pa did not have to buy these things.

Pa spent $1.25 on 5 pounds of powder for his gun, 60¢ on 15 pounds of lead, and $1 on 10 pounds of shot.

So altogether, Pa spent $461.97, which is more money than I ever heard of in my life. But that won't be all, neither—Pa's guidebook says that if you buy food along the way, it costs a deal more money than back east, and that most times when you cross a river you have to pay for a ferry. It costs $5 for the wagon, and if you want to ferry the oxen, that's 50¢ a head. So a smart man like my Pa will be sure to have plenty of money when he sets out to cross the Plains.

DAY 6 MAY 4

St. Joseph, Missouri

Our company is all got together and I have my new hat. Pa and the other men had a meeting to choose who would be the captain. Pa and Ma are glad it is an Iowa man, Captain Stewart. The men made an agreement about sharing the watch and minding the stock, and other chores on the trail. One lady, Mrs. Williams, said to Ma that they would be bound to end by fighting as she knew some of the men were quick-tempered and too handy with their fists. Our goal is to make 20 miles every day, but Pa says this will be a hard task. Well, now we set off on our journey across the Plains. "On our way rejoicing," as Ma said, although I don't think this was what she really meant as she was acting very cross. Here's what it's like on the trail. We rise before dawn, and I help Pa to cut out our oxen from the herd and drive them to the wagon to be hitched up. After breakfast, off we go, wagons well spread out along the way. Pa walks along beside the oxen, and I follow at the rear of the party, herding the milk cows. We wear cloths over our faces because the wagons make so much dust. Mrs. Williams was right about the men of this party. Some of

Below is a picture of an ox yoke. One yoke of oxen means two beasts. Our wagon is pulled by four yoke of oxen, so that makes eight oxen.

them must be the champion swearers of the world.

Most times Ma walks along beside the wagon so that she can look out for fuel. There is not much to be had on the Plains except buffalo chips, which she does not like but must gather into a big sack and save to make a fire. Ma and Sarah take turns to sit in the wagon and mind Martha.

A good morning's drive begins at seven, and we go along till noon, when we lay by for an hour or so. Pa unhitches the oxen and lets them graze, and we eat a meal. Pa and Ma would like to lay by all day on the Sabbath, but we cannot always do it, so we have a Bible reading at noon time. If we can stop, we sing hymns, and in the afternoon Ma sits in her rocking chair and writes letters home.

Yesterday we saw our first Indians. We went across their toll bridge, and the cost was six bits. Some of the Indians wear only a blanket, and many have their faces painted in stripes and spots, with brass rings round their arms and beads round their necks.

Every morning a man blows a horn like this one to tell the company to roll the wagons.

Here's a picture of Captain Stewart's compass. It's a sundial, too, so you can tell the time as well as which way you are going.

The Company

Most of the men in our company are farmers, but Mr. Parker is a shoemaker, who will set up his trade in Oregon, Mr. Burrell is a tailor, Mr. Draper a silversmith, Mr. Royce a lawyer, and there is the Rev. Minto. Ma is pleased there is a minister along. There is no doctor in our party, but Pa says there is one in the company ahead. There is a whole heap of children, and another boy, George, who minds the stock for his Pa. He is 11 years old—one year older than me.

THE BIG BLUE

CAPTAIN STEWART aimed to cross the Big Blue River where there was no ferry, so Pa and the other men had to find the tightest wagon bed and make a ferry out of that. Then all hands helped pull everything out of the wagons and take them to pieces. Some of the men swam over the river with a strong rope, with the wagon bed "ferry" tied onto it. The rope was stretched over the river and the ferry made to go from side to side by men hauling on either end of the rope. The goods or boards from the wagons were taken across a little at a time, with women and children last. Then the cattle and horses were herded down the bank and swum across. Pa heard that four cattle and a mule were drowned yesterday and a wagon washed away, but today the weather was fine and all went well. Martha fell into the river but was not much hurt.

All the party had to be got across, so a great deal of time was taken. When Pa's wagon crossed, he had much to do to mend it again, so Ma said she would go a ways down the bank and do some washing. George's Ma went to join her, and the other ladies did the same, until all you could see was piles of clothes and washtubs. We took off our dirty clothes, and then we had to put the new clothes on wet, but they soon dried.

Making Soap

Before setting out on this journey, Ma made a whole 10 pounds of soap for washing our clothes and for washing us. She put wood ashes into a big hopper, poured water over them, and collected the liquid—called lye—in the trough underneath.

Ma put the lye into boiling fat and stirred and stirred all day until the soap came. Then she poured it into tubs and stored it on the wagon. Most times Ma has to wash the clothes in cold water, because there is no hot water to be had, and this makes her very cross.

A Storm

By the end of the day, we were all on the far side of the river. Then a great storm of rain and hail began, so that Ma could not make a fire. We had only crackers to eat, and no coffee. In the morning the wagon was surrounded by so much water, you could almost fancy yourself in the river. Pa found the harness was muddy and needed a good clean.

The rain kept up all day. Several times we were stuck in the mud and could not move. In the evening, the wind was too high to raise a fire. More crackers to eat. Thunderstorm all night and a neighbor's ox struck by lightning. Very miserable indeed.

Crossing the River

There are plenty of different ways to cross a river. Sometimes you have to take the ferry—even if you swim your stock across, you have to pay for the wagon, and we have heard of folks paying as much as $16 to cross rivers in the west. Or if there is a bridge, you will have to pay to walk over that, too. Maybe you can make a raft, but if the river is strong you might be swept away in the water, and your wagon besides. If an ox or mule starts to kick and jump about, you'd best get out of his way as fast as you can.

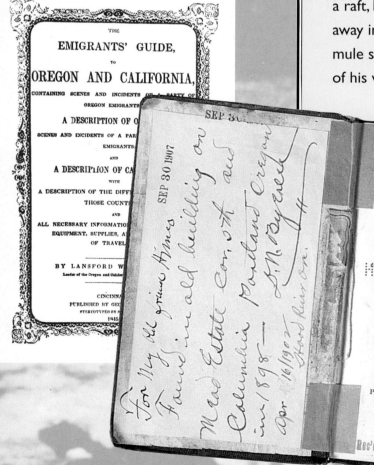

Pa likes to read guidebooks to learn about Oregon and how to get there. But he's mighty careful which ones he chooses—he's heard that some folks set down and write a guidebook that never made the journey themselves.

ASH HOLLOW

MA is awake the first of all of us, before sunrise. She gets the fuel ready, then she gets two forked sticks and drives them into the ground each side of the fire, lays a pole across, and swings the kettle upon it to heat the water. She has a deal of trouble to raise the fire most days because the wood is damp—in any case, it takes near an hour to bake the bread, warm the beans, fry the bacon, and boil the coffee. Even Martha drinks coffee, because most all of the water on the trail is bad. It's called poison or alkali water, and if a man drinks it, or an ox, he surely will perish.

I wait till Sarah has milked the cows and beg a drink of her when she brings the pails. I have to feed the hens. George says it's women's work and brags that his Ma don't ask him to do no such chores. But Pa says that I can help him on the farm all the time when we get to Oregon.

There's no table or nothing like it—most of the folks eat their meals sitting on the ground or a stump if they can find it, which is not much on the high Plains, for there are no trees to be seen.

After breakfast, Ma and Sarah wash the tinware and then pack up, while I help Pa with the stock. It's all hurry and bustle to get things in order. "Don't stand with your hands in your pockets, come and help me with these cattle! The devil's in them, for they will not be yoked." That's what Pa says most every morning nowadays.

These are Ma's cast-iron skillets and her little pan for making popcorn.

Sarah and me think the coffee tastes horrid, even more if the water is brackish. But we don't fuss Ma for lemonade, for we know there is none to be had.

Making Johnnycake

Of all the ladies in our party, my Ma makes the finest johnnycake. This here is her recipe:

1 cup of boiling water
½ cup of cornmeal
1 teaspoon of salt
Butter, if there is any to be had

The first thing to do is to mend the fire and make sure you have plenty of fuel to hand. Then add the salt to the cornmeal and pour on the water slowly. Stir as hard as you can so you don't get no lumps, then spread the mixture ⅓ inch deep in a shallow, buttered pan. It doesn't matter if you've only got small pans, like Ma uses to make muffins or biscuits—you can just put in spoonfuls instead, and get little johnnycakes. Dot the mixture with little bits of butter, and bake over the fire until crisp.

Ma says you must excuse her as she can't give you any notion of how long it takes—if it rains or your pots fall into the fire, you'll have trouble enough, though after a few weeks a crust of ash on your bread does not signify much. Let us hope your Ma is not a swearing woman, anyhow.

CHIMNEY ROCK

UNCLE Wesley Starr gave me a fishing line before we set out on our journey, but there's little fishing to be had on the Plains. Twice I caught a catfish in the Big Blue, which Ma cooked for supper, and George's father told me there will be salmon when we get west. He says there's hundreds, and they leap right out of the river into your hand.

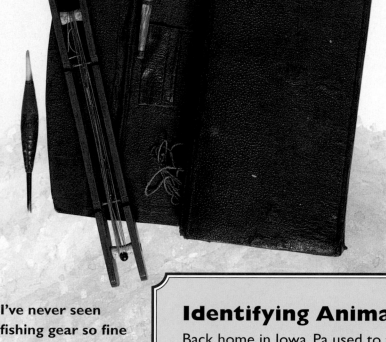

I've never seen fishing gear so fine as this, but have not been able to use it much. I hope there's some good fishing to be had in Oregon.

Going Hunting

Pa is a crack shot and has brought us rabbits, prairie chickens, and once, an antelope. I never ate antelope meat before, but it tasted pretty good.

My friend George bragged, "My Pa carries a brace of pistols and a bowie knife. Ain't that bloodcurdling?"

I said, "Then I hope he don't wound himself." Pa is the greatest buffalo hunter on the road, and George's Pa never killed one buffalo yet.

Buffalo!

All the men say we must get along, but if someone shouts "Buffalo!" they rush to fetch their guns and saddle their horses. Ma and the other ladies say it is a waste of shot, for they fire their guns without effect, and if they kill, the meat is mostly left to the birds. But I think it is fine sport to see a great chase over the Plains, and I wish I was a man so I could ride along with them. They always come back to

Identifying Animal Tracks

Back home in Iowa, Pa used to tell me stories about Indians and mountain men, the best hunters who ever lived. Now I can tell the difference between the tracks of a coyote, a prairie dog, a buffalo, and a grizzly bear. See if you can guess which is which. (I've given you the answers, just in case you can't figure it out.)

Buffalo

Grizzly Bear

Coyote

Prairie Dog

the camp in a jolly party, singing all the way. This time Pa did bring some meat, and we had buffalo steaks for supper. He brought a buffalo tongue besides, which Ma hung up to dry.

After we ate, I cleaned the guns while Pa went to see the stock. Our ox Sam has sore feet. Pa cut up a piece of rawhide and made boots for him, to help him along.

Indians are the bravest buffalo hunters around. When buffalo gallop, all you see is a great black cloud thundering toward you.

Pa's guns. He uses the shotgun [top] for small birds and animals, and the rifle for buffalo, antelope, and elk.

FORT LARAMIE

THIS morning George and I were at the back of the train when Sarah came running through the dust and told us they could see the watchtowers of Fort Laramie up ahead. About half a mile on we saw firearms shining in the distance, and then the blue coats of the cavalrymen.

The fort was full of Indians and mountain men who'd come with furs to make a trade. Ma went into the sutler's store and came out saying she was thankful that our bacon and flour had kept, as all the goods were very dear. She had to buy some sugar, though—75 cents for a pound! She posted a letter to Aunt Nancy Starr, and some men got hire of the forge for a time, and Pa put new shoes on Fan, the sorrel mare.

When we left the fort, we passed a village of Sioux Indians. The women came up round the wagons. They held up moccasins and lariats which they wanted to trade for bread, so Pa obliged them with some crackers. They asked Ma if she would trade her umbrella, but she would not.

Later, Pa let Sarah and I have a crack of the whip. Ma said it wasn't a ladylike thing for a girl to do, though I

Pa traded for these moccasins and gave them to Martha. Ma said the Indian women must be good workers to make such fine things.

This Indian bag was sewn from a cavalryman's boot. Ma said, "I wonder what happened to the poor cavalryman."

could see that Sarah liked it well enough. Martha fell out of the wagon, but was not much hurt.

Seeing the Elephant

At the fort, Pa and Ma met some go-backers. One man had all his stock stolen by Indians, and another's wife and children had died from cholera, so he broke up his wagon to make coffins, left his company, and headed back east on his horse. Pa said, "They have seen the elephant!" and Ma was very quiet. She is afraid because we have passed more graves than I could count on the road from St. Joseph, and cholera is the reason for it.

I'll bet you don't know what it meant when Pa said about "seeing the elephant." It means that if an overlander has a heap of problems, he is like to decide that life on the trail is too tough to take, and he will turn his wagon right round and head back home. Those people will tell you that only a madman would venture across the Plains, but my Pa knows better than to mind this sort of talk.

Ma said the sutler's store had so many articles it was almost as good as the stores back east.

At Fort Laramie you can have pictures made called daguerreotypes to send home to your folks.

Making Bullets

Some folk bought bullets at the fort, but Pa makes his own. To make musket balls for his rifle, Pa heats lead over the fire in an iron ladle. Then he pours the lead into the mold and waits for it to get hard before opening up the mold again. Here's a picture of Pa's powder flask and bullet mold.

DAY 61

JUNE 28

PLATTE RIVER

MANY of our party took sick with cholera, as Ma feared they might. She tended them this night with the other ladies. She gave them some medicine of laudanum and whiskey, but it did not make them well, so we can travel no further until they be buried. Ma said not to drink the water because it brings the sickness. So we obeyed her and stayed away from the well holes, but I thought I should die from thirst, so took a drink from the river. I heard a man say you will not catch the sickness if it is running water. I think

he said right, as I did not have a fever nor a vomit, nor shiver and shake as people do who have the cholera. We see other wagon trains hurry past as quick as they can, for fear of it. A doctor came to us from another company, and I heard him tell Ma he has tended 40 sufferers this day.

Death on the Trail

Ma said this road is like a graveyard—in some places it is five or six in a row, with wooden crosses and stones to mark the place. George's Pa died in the

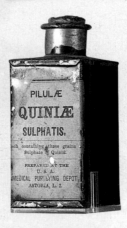

Some folk took sick with malaria and had to take a special medicine called quinine.

The Donner Party

I guess there isn't one person in the world who hasn't heard of the Donner party, but in case you're a greenhorn and don't know, I'll tell you: They were bound for California. They should have started their journey in April, but they didn't begin till the end of May because they were too busy loading their wagons with fancy articles. Then they took a cutoff that was no shortcut at all and got trapped in the mountains of the Sierra Nevada over winter. Their food supplies ran out, so they ate all their animals, and then fur, harness, cloth… I heard they even ate their dead companions, as savages do, just to keep themselves alive! Nobody could fetch them out until February, and then they were half mad. And as Ma says, there's a moral to that story: Never take no cutoffs, and hurry along just as fast as you can.

night, and must be buried with the others. His Ma is half crazy from fear that the wolves will dig him up and eat him, for we have seen this happen. And sometimes the Indians will dig a man up for his clothes, and will not cover him again.

The men took boards from the wagons to make coffins and buried the dead. The minister was buried with the rest, but we sang the hymn "Nearer, My God, to Thee" and Captain Stewart spoke a few words.

Now Pa has the cholera. Mr. Williams sent for the doctor, for Mrs. Williams was ill besides Pa, and several others as well. Ma was all day in the wagon with him, and I could do nothing, but went and sat by myself away from the camp. I don't want Pa to die, but can scarcely believe he will live. Sarah said we must pray, so we did. Then Sarah asked me, was I much frighted. I did not say yes, but it was true. If Pa dies, I'm afraid we will be left here alone on the Plains.

Healing the Sick

The doctor carries a case like this one, full of medicines. He gives them to people, but most times they do not do any good. One of the ladies in the next company lost her husband and four children. Only the baby was left.

INDEPENDENCE ROCK

All the wagons were gathered in a circle by the Rock, and this is where we had our celebration.

Some folks carve their names on the rock, others paint them, and some mark them in axle grease.

MY Pa was real sick, but after some days the doctor said Pa would be well. Ma said, "Thank the Lord for a miracle!" And it *is* a miracle, because even a strong man like my Pa may get sick with the cholera and die in one day.

The next day Ma drove the wagon. Then she said I may take a turn— the first time I ever drove the oxen, but made out pretty well—and so we went on through the day. And shall continue, until Pa is strong again.

Now it is the Fourth of July. Hurrah boys, hurrah! And we have reached Independence Rock, which was Captain Stewart's plan, so it pleases him well. There will be a dance tonight, as one of the company is a fiddler, and Ma and the other ladies have saved goods enough for a feast. Ma says we have cause to celebrate as Pa grows stronger each day. When he knew how Ma and I shared driving the oxen, he said it was a man's work I had done and he was pleased with me. He says we have traveled over 800 miles since we left St. Joseph.

George and I climbed up the rock. There are thousands of names carved on it. We wrote our names and the date. I saw my Uncle Henry Adams's name that he put on in 1849 when he traveled across the Plains. Aunt Betsy Adams got sick with the measles and died on the journey, but Uncle Henry got a big farm in Oregon and married another lady, so he ended happy.

My sister Sarah helped Ma and the other ladies to sew this flag.

Celebration Time

Pa said he will try his hand at hunting again. Ma would have stopped him if she could, but he went out with the other men and killed an elk.

Ma and the other ladies brought their scrap bags out of the wagons and sewed an American flag, which looked pretty good. We all sang, *"Cheer up, brothers, as we go Oe'r the mountains, westward ho Where the herds of deer and buffalo Furnish the fare."* Then the men fired their guns and all shouted "Hurrah for Oregon!"

All together, it was a fine time, though I never saw mosquitoes so bad as there are here, and everyone has bites. As for the sun, wind, and dust, we are all in the same way with split lips and smarting eyes.

Ma had some potatoes from an Indian, and she made a pie with dried tomatoes, and there was cake, too.

Singing Songs

Sarah's and my favorite song is "Clementine." Here are the words:

*In a cavern, in a canyon
Excavating for a mine,
Dwelt a miner, forty-niner,
And his daughter, Clementine.*

*Light she was and like a fairy,
And her shoes were number nine,
Herring boxes without topses
Sandals were for Clementine.*

*Drove she ducklings to the water,
Every morning just at nine
Put her foot against a splinter,
Fell into the foaming brine.*

*Ruby lips above the water,
Blowing bubbles soft and fine
But, alas, I was no swimmer,
So I lost my Clementine.*

*In my dreams she still doth haunt me
Robed in garments soaked in brine,
Though in life, I used to kiss her
Now she's dead, I draw the line.*

Chorus:
*Oh my darling, oh my darling, oh my darling Clementine!
Thou art lost and gone forever, dreadful sorry, Clementine.*

DAY
68
JULY
5

DEVIL'S GATE

WE passed the Devil's Gate today. Pa says it is a wonder, because the Sweetwater River has made a gap in the solid rock. He is happy because there is good grass for the stock. I went to fetch some water for Ma. The water here is better than the Platte, which is muddy and full of wigglers, which, in case you don't know, are tiny little bugs. A band of Indians came into our camp. Pa swapped hard bread with them for good berries and traded a shirt and a sewing needle for more potatoes. The Indians offered to trade for Ma's umbrella, but still she would not. Two of them shot at a mark with Pa's gun, then Pa took his turn and he beat them.

Ma made a pie with the potatoes and some elk meat that was left over from yesterday's feast.

The camp was quite surrounded by Indians last night. Pa said we must take care that the stock is safe, for he

Here are some arrowheads I found on the trail.

The first time we saw parties of Indians dressed like this, we thought they might attack us, but they were only going to fight each other.

had heard of a man who slept with his horse's reins tied to his arm at night, but when he awoke in the morning— no horse! But Pa says that Indians are not bad people. Uncle Henry Adams was rescued by Shoshone Indians when he fell into the Snake River, and a lot of folk can tell you stories of how they would have starved but for the Indians giving them berries and roots.

Ma said she would lie awake all night thinking we would be killed, but I found my scalp on in the morning, and so did the rest of the company.

Most Indians have guns, but they use bows and arrows like these, too.

A Cheyenne Game

An Indian boy showed me this game. It took a deal of time to learn it because I could not speak a word of his language, nor he mine except to say "white man." Here's how it goes:

First, get four flat sticks and mark them each a different color with earth or leaves or such like. Then give them numbers, one to four. Leave three sticks plain on the back and score three black lines on the back of the fourth. Now go and find yourself 12 pebbles for counters.

Throw the sticks into the air. Add up the numbers on the sticks, and take that number of pebbles for yourself. If a stick lands plain side up, that don't count. If the black lines land face up, you get no points at all, no matter what the other sticks say. If you throw the sticks and score no points, you must hand them over to the next person. Then he does the same, and so on. If there ain't no more pebbles for him, then he must take them from you. The one who wins is the first to get all 12 pebbles into his hand.

Pa does not play cards, but some of the men in our party take any chance to have a game. Pa likes to smoke, and this here is his pipe and a twist of tobacco.

SOUTH PASS

WE are up so high, yet we barely noticed we were climbing. The way we took was not like mountains at all. It is July, and hot in the daytime, but in the morning there is ice on the water buckets. It is a strange place.

We hoped Ma would forget about lessons if we minded her and did our chores, but when we stopped this noon she said just because we're traveling, there's no need to turn into savages, and it was time for a little schooling. The schoolbooks had a good soaking when we crossed the Sweetwater River so they are quite spoiled (Oh, what sadness!),

but that didn't stop Ma. First she held a spelling bee, and Sarah beat me. Then we had a competition to see how many Bible verses we could remember, and Sarah bested me in that, too. Ma gave Sarah a piece of chocolate for a prize. She'd kept it by her all the way from Iowa, and it wasn't spoiled! Sarah shared the chocolate with me, though she didn't have to. Then Ma gave us some figuring, and we took turns to use the slate. When Pa came back from his meeting with Captain Stewart and the others, Ma asked him what we might do for our geography. Pa told us about Soda Springs, farther up the trail. The water bubbles up and

Ma packed some of Martha's toys in the wagon, but she keeps dropping them out and they must be got back.

Ma packed our slate and schoolbooks. The slate pencil is like a stick. Sarah puts her hands to her ears when I write on the slate. She does not like the squeak.

tickles your nose, and if you add sugar to it, it is as sweet as lemonade. Then he told about Steamboat Springs, where the water comes out of the ground so hot that Ma will have only to pour it on the coffee, and it will be made. He said, that's geography enough for anyone, ain't it?

One of Ma's cows died. Nobody knows why. It must be from drinking alkali water, which Pa says is very bad hereabouts. Pa and Ma came to look at the poor beast, and forgot Martha. Sarah thought she was with Mrs. Williams in their wagon, but at our next halt we found she was not there, and nobody could find her. Then another company came up, and there was Martha sitting in a wagon! They'd found her in the road. Ma was mighty glad to see her.

Sarah's Accident

We were journeying along in the afternoon, and Sarah jumped down from the wagon as she has done many times before without upset. But this time, her dress became tangled on the axle handle, and she was caught up and tipped over. Pa heard her shout, but could not stop the oxen, and the wagon wheel ran over her and broke her leg into pieces. Pa ran to pick her up, and Ma cried, "Oh my poor child, what shall we do?"

Pa has sent ahead for the doctor in the next train. It is but two miles ahead. Ma fixed a couch for Sarah in the wagon with the featherbed. It jolts so that it pains her a great deal, and she cannot help but weep. Ma sat by her a long time, very quiet, and then I heard her pray, "May the Lord give us the strength to endure such hardships."

Ma wrote to Aunt Nancy Starr about the accident, but won't be able to mail that letter until we get to Oregon.

**DAY
123
AUGUST
29**

SNAKE RIVER PLAIN

AFTER leaving Fort Hall, we said farewell to those of our party who were bound for California and traveled along the south bank of the Snake River for days before we headed for Fort Boise. Since, we have crossed the Boise River, the Snake, and the Malheur, losing no small part of our goods, which were swept away by the current.

Now we must travel through a kind of desert until we come to the Blue Mountains. There is almost no water to be had for man or beast. Pa told Ma to lighten our wagon—throw away anything you do not need, because the oxen are weak and may not get over the mountains. So Ma threw away her rocking chair and our clock, though she was sorry to do it. Others in our party have discarded cooking stoves, plows, grindstones, spades, trunks, and boxes of all kinds.

Each day the oxen grow weaker and our progress slower. Yesterday our ox Tip dropped dead suddenly, in the

Plenty of folks are throwing goods out of their wagons to lighten them. We have seen fancy articles of all sorts along the road, even a small piano.

yoke. Sarah wept, and said, "Pity the poor ox who has helped us on our way and gave us his very last step," and Ma looked sad. Pa said he will harness the mare Fan instead.

Many in our company have lost their cattle, which lie dead on this road. There is no end to the abandoned yokes to be seen, as well as some splendid good wagons, just left to stand. But at least they will give us wood enough to raise a fire. Some of the bones have writing on them with messages about where good water is to be found, and such like.

Tonight we will have meat, the first for five days. Our ox Tip is to be turned into supper for us and many more besides. Ma has just enough water left in our cans to make coffee. We thought we should have none for the morning, but a friendly Indian came to the camp and showed Captain Stewart where to find water, so we took the cattle to the place to drink, and I filled the cans for Ma.

Packing

If you have lost all your stock and no one can help you, then there is nothing for it but you must pack to Oregon. This means you must pick up as many of your goods as you can carry and make your way walking.

FLAGSTAFF HILL

We have used up most all of the candles for our lantern, but Ma says she will make more directly we are set down in Oregon.

WE stopped this night in one spot, but another company had visited before us, and it was dirty. The stench was such that Ma said, "I should as soon think of keeping house in a barnyard," and the other ladies said they would not stay. So on we went to another camp. Pa said that we might get a look at the Blue Mountains from this place, and so we did.

Captain Stewart guided the wagons into a circle, then we had our chores to do before nightfall. Pa and I unyoked the oxen and gave them water. They must have grazing, but there is very little grass to be had here, only sagebrush. Poor Fan looks thin and sick. Pa thinks she may not live long.

There is not much food to be had, but George's Ma had some pie saved, which she swapped for some of Ma's dried fruit, so we ate it for supper. Afterwards, Pa smoked his pipe and Ma mended some clothes. The doctor said Sarah's leg might not heal for a long time, but she is not so sick now as she was. She asked Ma if she might have her nine-patch quilt so

The finest time of day is when Ma makes supper because George and I can go off to play and run races.

that she could sew, too. I went to watch the men playing cards. Some of them had a bet on how many miles we had traveled and began to quarrel, then one knocked another down with his whipstock. Pa saw it and said, "Now, boys!" and he and Mr. Williams went to stop the fight. Ma said it was caused by whiskey and it wasn't the first time, neither.

Before Sarah's leg was broke, we used to sleep together in a tent, and we'd tell stories about our new home in Oregon. Now Sarah sleeps in the wagon with Ma and Martha, and Pa sleeps in the tent with me. Sometimes it is nice to sleep outside, but not tonight, because it is as cold as winter, though it is only August.

Keeping Guard

Every night the wagons are set in a circle to make the camp safe and shelter us from the wind, although if it blows up a storm you are still like to get your head blown off and a good soaking besides.

Pa has to help guard the camp at night—the men take turns to do this. I want to help them, but Pa says I am not old enough. They have to protect the stock from wolves and thieves. One man shot his own mule in mistake for an Indian, because it was moving about in the dark. But if the cattle take fright and there is a stampede, there is little any man can do to stop it.

Last week the stock charged through the camp and smashed all in their path, and Mr. Burrell's wife and her baby were trampled over and afterward died. No one knows what caused the stampede. Mr. Burrell said it was Indians and that he would kill the next one he sees, but Captain Stewart talked to him, and after he said he would not.

DAY
131
SEPTEMBER 6

BLUE MOUNTAINS

NOW we are come right into the mountains. Yesterday we made only ten miles, and I thought it as bad as could be, but this land is even worse. Rocky, slippery, and muddy, up and down the hills, some so steep that the poor cattle cannot pull the wagons, which must be winched up from the top. The winch is made from an empty wagon standing at the top of the hill, with one set of wheels turning free and a strong rope from the axle fixed to the wagon below. At the signal, the men and oxen turn the wheels with all their strength to drag that wagon up the hill. When our wagon was halfway up, it hit the end of a log and the rope was loosed so that it jolted all the way down again, and Sarah was inside it all the time. Ma was much frighted and climbed down the hill as fast as she could. All thought the wagon would be broke in half and Sarah with it, but it got stuck on a big tree, and the only damage was a torn canvas. Sarah was much hurt and I heard her cry out, but she is safe.

Now we are come to a broad gully, and Captain Stewart aims to lower each of the cattle on ropes, one by one. Most all of the cattle are weak and ailing and will not make much struggle.

Tonight, a great rainstorm. Ma baked bread for supper by standing for near two hours holding an umbrella over the fire. Pa said he was mighty glad she had not traded it with an Indian. Ma said, "All this for Oregon," and shook her head.

When Pa saw so many wagons overturned and broken in pieces he said to Captain Stewart that he had figured that crossing the mountains would be the hardest part of the journey, but "This beats all!"

Descending into Green River Valley

Trouble with the Wagon

Yesterday the horn sounded at seven o'clock and we began, but after a mile one of our wheels shed its iron tire, and there was nothing for it but to stop and mend it. Pa had to make the wooden rim of the wheel larger, so that the tire could be fit back again tight enough around it, so he cut small pieces of wood into curven shapes and nailed them round the edge of the wheel to make it into a bigger circle. Then he heated the tire and fit it back on the wheel. I fetched a bucket of water, and he threw it on the wheel.

The cold water made the hot iron smaller so that it fit tighter round the wood. Mr. Parker had some tools which he lent Pa, then Pa returned the favor when Mr. Parker broke the axle of his wagon by driving over a big stone. Mr. Parker carried a spare axle in his wagon, which was well, for it would take a longer time than we can spare to find a tree and cut it down. If your wagon wheel sheds its tire, that is trouble enough for any man, but if a wheel breaks, there is no remedy but to get another.

OREGON CITY

WELL, we made it to Oregon City! Captain Stewart said we should travel by the Barlow Road across the Cascade Mountains so that we might avoid ferrying down the Columbia River, and most of the men agreed. On this road we passed some families who had lost everything and were obliged to pack the rest of the journey—a poor-looking set all together. But many of our company were not much better.

Our team is now made of six oxen (our ox Blue died last week), Pa's mare, and Ma's last cow. But we have traveled almost 2,000 miles, and it is near five and a half months since we left our home in Iowa.

By the final week, most all of our food was gone, for Ma had given much to those who had nothing but strips of meat cut from dead oxen. At the last, she discovered that the little bacon we had left was turned bad and could not be used. It will be mighty fine to have a good dinner again.

By the end of the journey, Sarah was real sick with a fever, and her leg pained her so that she has been taken into a house which was made a hospital. Ma fears that Sarah may never be well again—her fever is so bad that she does not know us.

Here are some folk arriving in Oregon City. Uncle Henry said it is like Paradise in the Bible. I guess I don't know about Paradise, for I never saw it, but Oregon City looks pretty good to me, anyhow.

HOME AT LAST!

SARAH'S fever broke after some days, and she got well again, so we were able to move to our new land on the west bank of the Willamette River. We built our house here, about 20 miles from Oregon City. I helped Pa cut down the trees and raise a log cabin, and the wagon was broken up to make furniture. We spread the wagon top across to make a roof for the first winter, but now we have a shingle roof, an iron stove, and a proper door instead of a buffalo hide. Pa says the land is good, and he intends putting out a large orchard.

Pa has promised Ma that he'll make her a new rocking chair as soon as ever he can put his hands on a fine piece of wood. Ma laughed when she heard him say it. It's strange to sleep in a house again, after such a time traveling, but I'm mighty glad that we made it to our new home.

Here's our fine new cabin, which I helped Pa build.

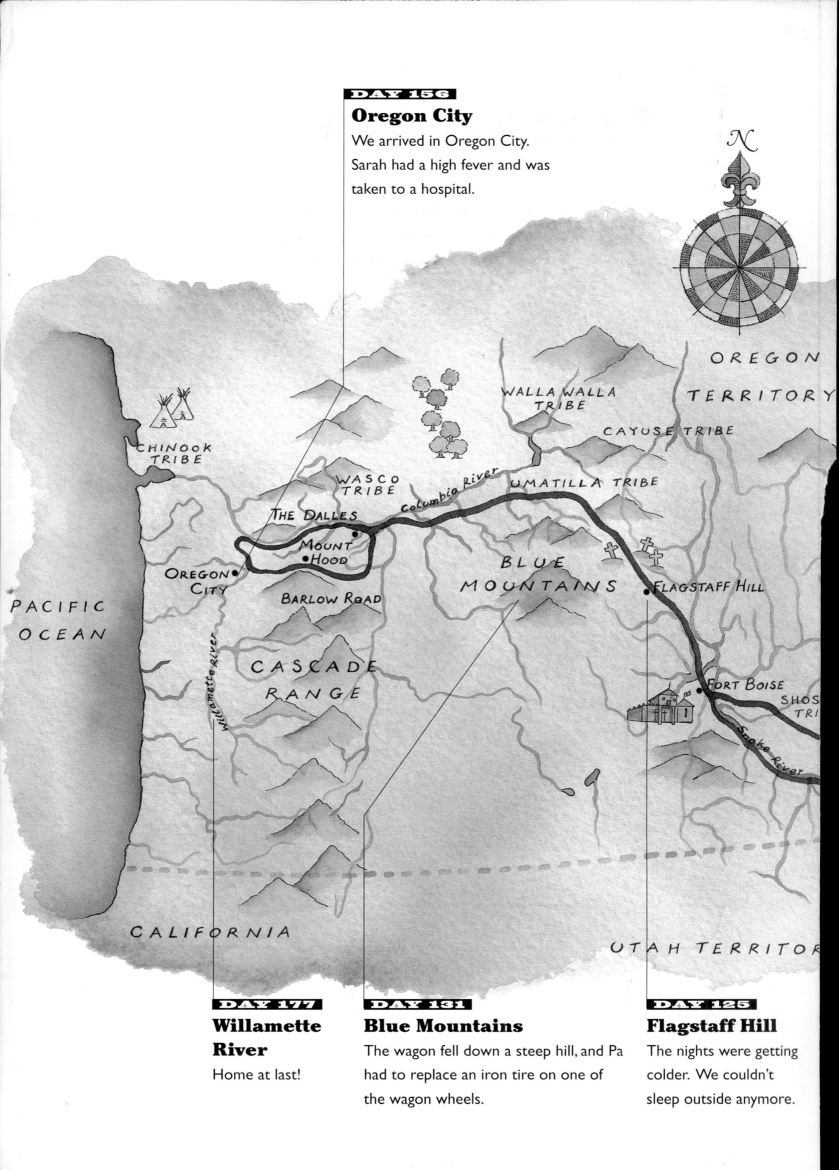

DAY 156

Oregon City

We arrived in Oregon City. Sarah had a high fever and was taken to a hospital.

N

OREGON TERRITORY

CHINOOK TRIBE

WALLA WALLA TRIBE

CAYUSE TRIBE

WASCO TRIBE

Columbia River

UMATILLA TRIBE

THE DALLES

MOUNT HOOD

BLUE MOUNTAINS

FLAGSTAFF HILL

OREGON CITY

BARLOW ROAD

PACIFIC OCEAN

Willamette River

CASCADE RANGE

FORT BOISE

SHOS TRI

Snake River

CALIFORNIA

UTAH TERRITOR

DAY 177

Willamette River

Home at last!

DAY 131

Blue Mountains

The wagon fell down a steep hill, and Pa had to replace an iron tire on one of the wagon wheels.

DAY 125

Flagstaff Hill

The nights were getting colder. We couldn't sleep outside anymore.

A Map of Jesse's Journey

The large map shows the places Jesse wrote about in his journal, with territorial boundaries as they were in 1852. The small map shows the Oregon Trail going through state boundaries as they exist today.

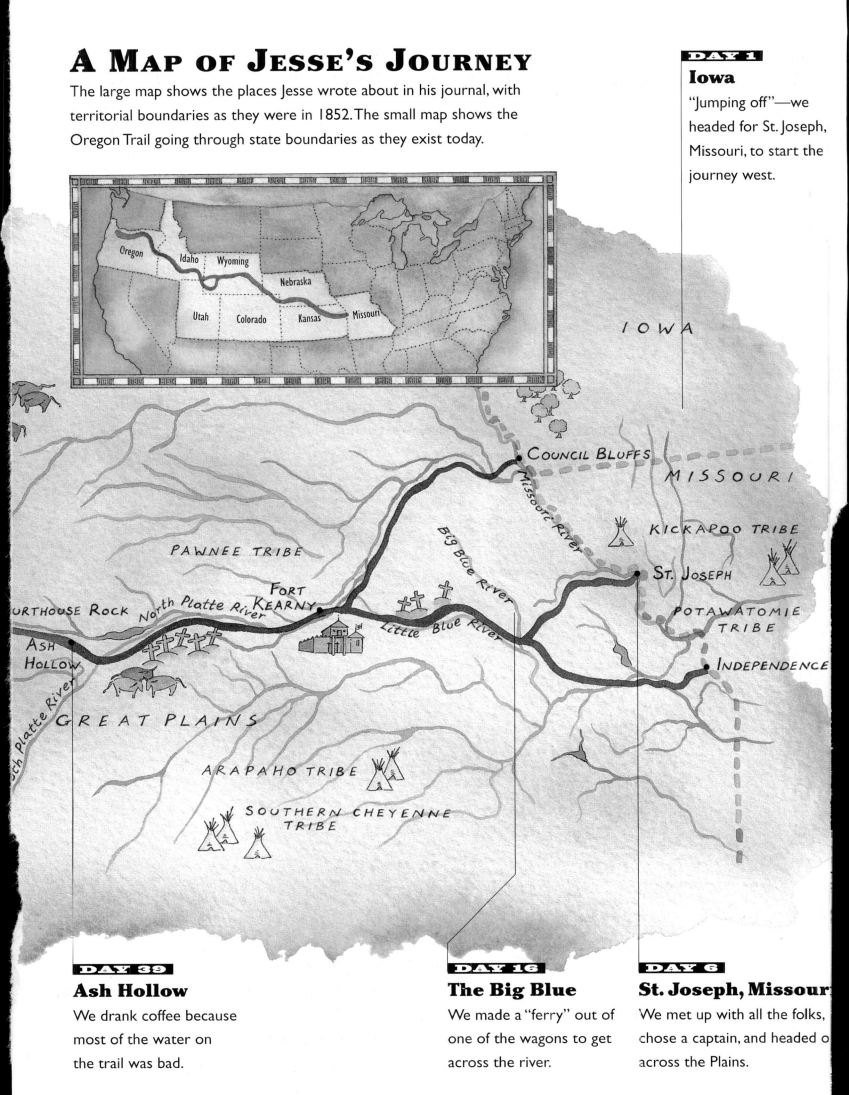

Oregon
Idaho   Wyoming
Nebraska
Utah   Colorado   Kansas   Missouri

IOWA

COUNCIL BLUFFS

MISSOURI

Missouri River

PAWNEE TRIBE

KICKAPOO TRIBE

St. JOSEPH

Big Blue River

FORT KEARNY

POTAWATOMIE TRIBE

URTHOUSE ROCK   North Platte River

Little Blue River

INDEPENDENCE

ASH HOLLOW

ch Platte River

GREAT PLAINS

ARAPAHO TRIBE

SOUTHERN CHEYENNE TRIBE

DAY 1
Iowa
"Jumping off"—we headed for St. Joseph, Missouri, to start the journey west.

DAY 39
Ash Hollow
We drank coffee because most of the water on the trail was bad.

DAY 16
The Big Blue
We made a "ferry" out of one of the wagons to get across the river.

DAY 6
St. Joseph, Missouri
We met up with all the folks, chose a captain, and headed o across the Plains.

AFTERWORD

IF you want to know what happened after my journal ended, here it is. Sarah's broken leg finally healed, which Ma said was the good air of Oregon, though Sarah did always walk crooked after that time.

Pa did well on his new farm, and prospered, and in due time Sarah and Martha found men to marry them, and did well in their turn.

A few months after we arrived in Oregon, my brother Abraham was born. When he had sense enough to understand, I told him about our journey across the Plains. He made me tell him over and over. When I told him how Pa was sick with the cholera and like to die, he said, "Weren't you frighted?" This time I said that I was the most afraid I have ever been, which was the truth. Then I told him about the Indians, and the animals, and all the different things to see, and he said, "Wasn't that the best adventure you ever had in your life?"

And it's true, it was. I've done many things in my life, and I have a farm of my own, with a wife and five children, but nothing comes to my recollection so thrilling as my journey on the Oregon Trail. If I'd been Pa or Ma, I fancy I'd have been half-crazy with fear most all of the time, for the hardships and danger, but I wasn't. I was ten years old, and I had the time of my life.

1882

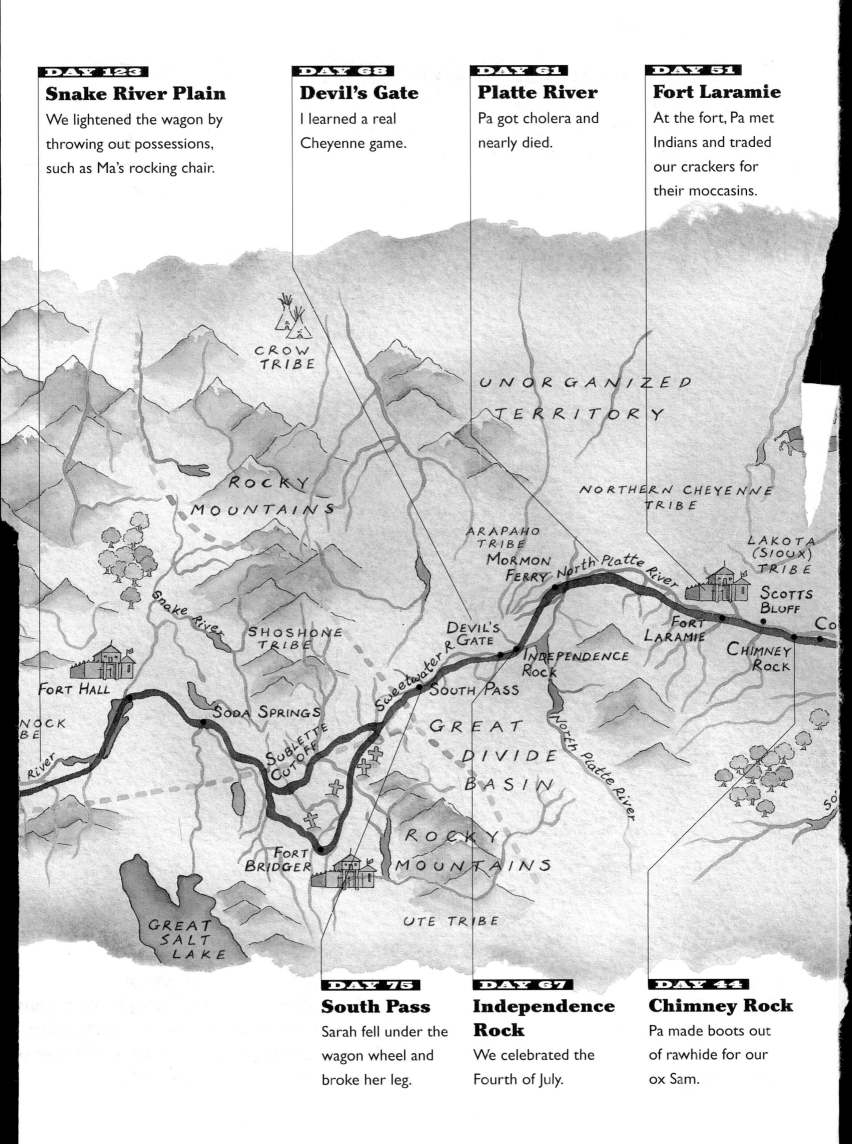

DAY 123

Snake River Plain

We lightened the wagon by throwing out possessions, such as Ma's rocking chair.

DAY 68

Devil's Gate

I learned a real Cheyenne game.

DAY 61

Platte River

Pa got cholera and nearly died.

DAY 51

Fort Laramie

At the fort, Pa met Indians and traded our crackers for their moccasins.

CROW TRIBE

UNORGANIZED TERRITORY

ROCKY MOUNTAINS

NORTHERN CHEYENNE TRIBE

ARAPAHO TRIBE

MORMON FERRY

North Platte River

LAKOTA (SIOUX) TRIBE

SHOSHONE TRIBE

Snake River

DEVIL'S R. GATE

SCOTTS BLUFF

FORT LARAMIE

Sweetwater R.

INDEPENDENCE Rock

SOUTH PASS

CHIMNEY Rock

Co

FORT HALL

NOCK BE

River

SODA SPRINGS

SUBLETTE CUTOFF

GREAT DIVIDE BASIN

North Platte River

So

FORT BRIDGER

ROCKY MOUNTAINS

UTE TRIBE

GREAT SALT LAKE

DAY 75

South Pass

Sarah fell under the wagon wheel and broke her leg.

DAY 67

Independence Rock

We celebrated the Fourth of July.

DAY 44

Chimney Rock

Pa made boots out of rawhide for our ox Sam.

INDEX

ACKNOWLEDGMENTS
Breslich & Foss would like to thank Paul Erickson, Helen Erickson, Eve Hocombe, Jim Murray, Katy Oliver, Janet Ravenscroft, Ted Rosner, and Michael Bad Hand Terry.

Picture Credits
Courtesy of Anschutz Collection: pp.18-19; Bancroft Library: (xffF850 P455) p.19 (bottom); Beinecke Rare Books and Manuscript Library, Yale University: p.30; Denver Public Library, Western Historical Collection: front cover, pp.8-9, pp.22-3; Mark Holt Collection: front cover, p.1, pp.6-7 (center); Henry E. Huntington Library, San Marino, California: p.11 (top right), p.20 (top), p.27, p.29 (bottom); Joslyn Art Museum, Nebraska: pp.16-17; National Archives: (69-N-19519) pp.6-7; Nebraska State Historical Society: pp.10-11; Photo by Ben Wittick, Courtesy Museum of New Mexico: Neg. No. 3038, pp.28-9, 30-31; Oregon Historical Society: p.8 (center), p.11 (center), p.32 (center), p.33 (top left); Stanford University Museum of Art, Gift of Jane L. Stanford: pp.26-7; Utah State Historical Society: pp.12-13; Walters Art Gallery, Baltimore: pp.2-3, p.15 (top right), pp.20-21.

All other photographs by Nigel Bradley and Miki Slingsby.

Maps by Lorraine Harrison.

BIBLIOGRAPHY
Faragher, John Mack. *Women and Men on the Overland Trail*. New Haven and London: Yale University Press, 1979.
Parkman, Francis. *The Oregon Trail*. New York: New American Library, 1950.
Schlissel, Lillian. *Women's Diaries of the Westward Journey*. New York: Schocken Books, 1982.
Unruh, John D., Jr. *The Plains Across: The Overland Emigrants and the Trans-Mississippi West, 1840–1860*. Urbana and Chicago: University of Illinois Press, 1982.